# Milton the Early Riser

BY ROBERT KRAUS

PICTURES BY JOSE ARUEGO AND ARIANE DEWEY

Aladdin Paperbacks

Aladdin Paperbacks
An imprint of Simon & Schuster
Children's Publishing Division
1230 Avenue of the Americas
New York, NY 10020

Manufactured in the United States of America

Library of Congress Cataloging in Publication Data
Kraus, Robert, 1925–
Milton the early riser / by Robert Kraus : pictures by Jose Aruego & Ariane Dewey
p.    cm.
Summary: The first one to awake, Milton the Panda tries hard to
wake all the other animals, but to no avail.
[1. Pandas—Fiction.]   I. Aruego, Jose, ill.   II. Dewey, Ariane,
ill.   III. Title.
PZ7.K868Mh    1987
[E]—dc19      87-32072   CIP   AC
ISBN 0-671-66272-4
ISBN 0-671-66911-7 pbk.

For
Pamela, Bruce, Billy,
and Juan

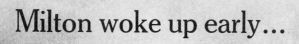

Milton woke up early...

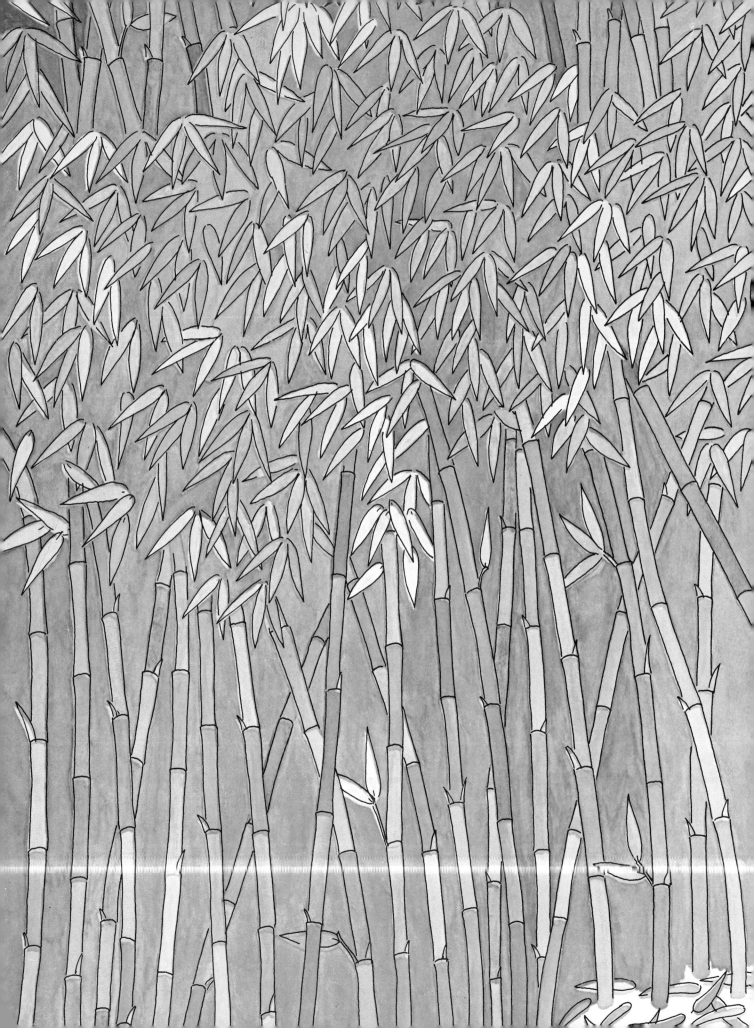

and went out to play.

But there was nobody to play with.

The Creeps next door were still asleep.

So were the Whippersnappers across the way

and the Nincompoops in the back.

# The whole world seemed to be asleep.

# So Milton watched television.

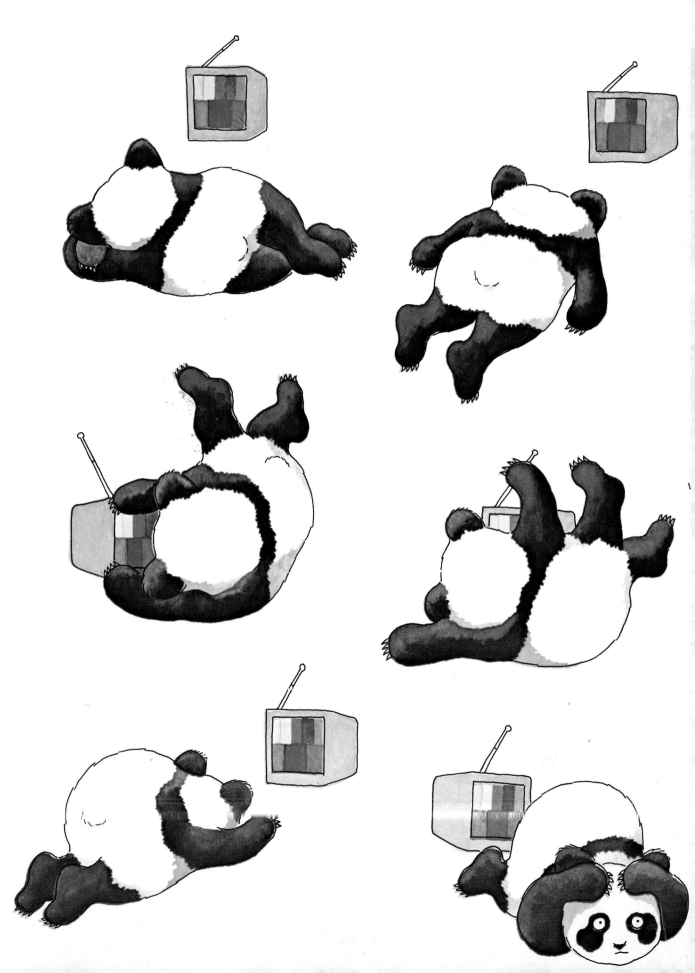

# And the sleepers slept on.

# Milton jumped up and down.

# But the sleepers slept on.

# Milton danced and did tricks.

Yet the sleepers slept on.

Then Milton sang up a storm.

The mountains shook.
The trees trembled.

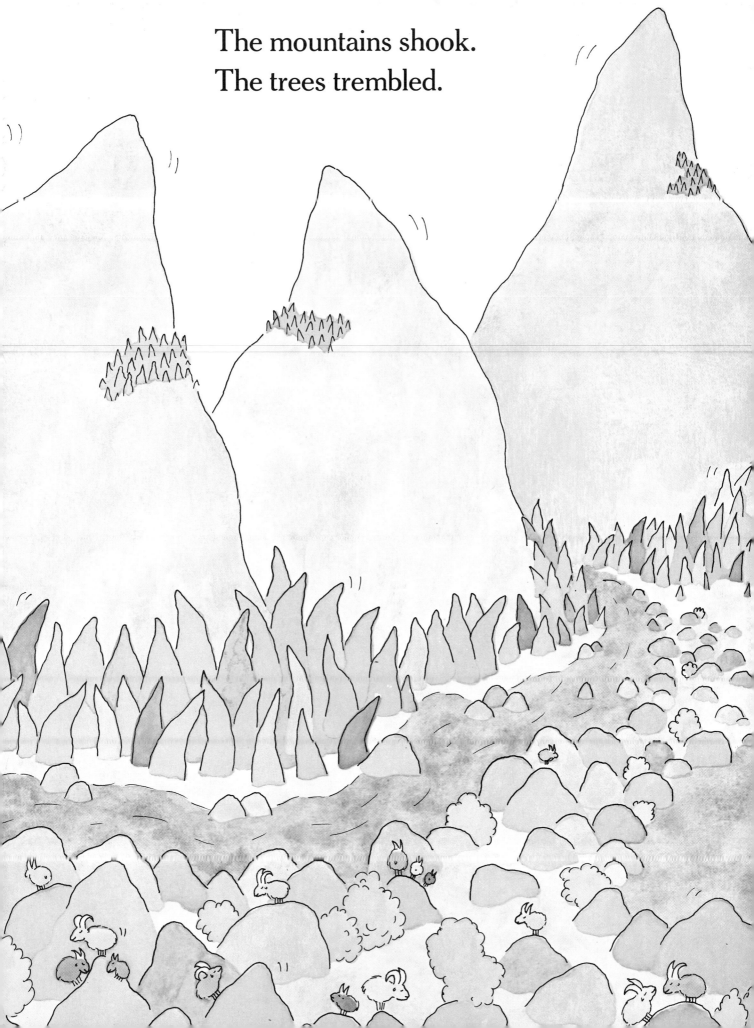

# And a whirlwind blew the sleepers out of bed!

Still the sleepers slept on.

"Oh dear," said Milton. "What a mess."

And he worked and worked
and he put things right.

Just as everybody woke up.

Everybody but Milton.

"Rise and shine," said Milton's father.
"Wake up sleepy-head," said Milton's mother.
Milton the early riser didn't hear a word.

He was fast asleep.